The
GLENELG
COUNTRY
SCHOOL

A
BIRTHDAY
· BOOK ·

· Presented in honor of ·

Marisa Caren Jack
on her seventh birthday

· Given by ·

Mom and Daddy
June 8, 2001

YOUNG CAM JANSEN
and the
Baseball Mystery
5

A Viking Easy-to-Read

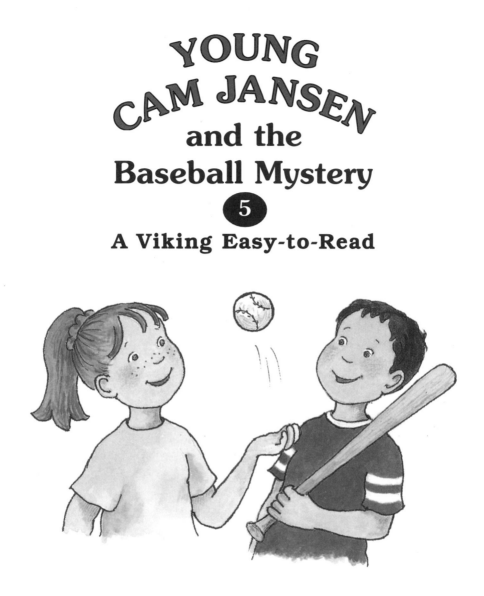

by David A. Adler
illustrated by Susanna Natti

VIKING

For Aliza, Uri, Dovid, Shlomo, and Ilana
—D. A.

To Emma Willsky
—S. N.

VIKING
Published by the Penguin Group
Penguin Putnam Books for Young Readers,
345 Hudson Street, New York, New York 10014, U.S.A.
Penguin Books Ltd, 27 Wrights Lane, London W8 5TZ, England
Penguin Books Australia Ltd, Ringwood, Victoria, Australia
Penguin Books Canada Ltd, 10 Alcorn Avenue, Toronto, Ontario, Canada M4V 3B2
Penguin Books (N.Z.) Ltd, 182-190 Wairau Road, Auckland 10, New Zealand

Penguin Books Ltd, Registered Offices: Harmondsworth, Middlesex, England

First published in 1999 by Viking, a member of Penguin Putnam Books for Young Readers.

3 5 7 9 10 8 6 4
Text copyright © David A. Adler, 1999   Illustrations copyright © Susanna Natti, 1999
All rights reserved

LIBRARY OF CONGRESS CATALOGING-IN-PUBLICATION DATA
Adler, David A.
Young Cam Jansen and the baseball mystery / by David A. Adler ; illustrated by Susanna Natti.
p. cm. — (A Viking easy-to-read)
Summary: When a baseball game is stopped because of a lost ball,
Cam uses her photographic memory to find the ball.
ISBN 0-670-88481-2 (hc)
[1. Balls (Sporting goods)—Fiction. 2. Baseball—Fiction.
3. Lost and found possessions—Fiction.]
I.Natti, Susanna, ill. II. Title. III. Series.
PZ7.A2615Yl 1999 [Fic]—dc21 98-35726 CIP AC

Printed in Singapore   Set in Bookman

CONTENTS

Cam Jansen has an amazing memory. Do you?

Look at this picture. Blink your eyes and say "Click." Then turn to the last page of this book

1. PLAY BALL!

"Watch out!"

Cam Jansen called

to her friend Eric Shelton.

"Watch out!"

"Why?" Eric asked.

They were walking in a park.

Splash!

Eric stepped into a puddle.

"That's why," Cam told him.

The park was crowded.

People were sitting on benches.

Some were reading.

Some were talking.

Some were resting.

Children were riding bicycles

and flying kites.

"Watch out!" Cam said again.

Eric looked down.

He wasn't about to step into a puddle.

"Why?" Eric asked.

Just then a red ball flew by.

It almost hit him.

"That's why," Cam told Eric.

"Watch out!" Cam said a third time.

A dog was playing catch

with an old man.

The dog almost ran into Eric.

It ran to the red ball.

The dog stopped the ball with its foot.

Then it picked up the ball in its teeth

and ran back with it.

Eric was careful.

He watched where he walked.

He didn't want to step into another puddle.

He watched the kites

and the children riding bicycles.

He didn't want anyone or anything

to knock into him.

Cam and Eric walked

to the edge of the baseball field.

"There's Robert," Cam said.

She pointed.

"And there's Rachel."

Robert and Rachel were on the baseball field.

Some of Cam and Eric's other friends

were there, too.

Eric said, "I hope they're not waiting for us."

Cam and Eric hurried to the baseball field.

"I'm glad you're here," Robert told them.

"I brought a bat."

"And I brought a ball," Rachel said.

"But we still don't have enough players."

Robert said, "A lot of people

told me they would come.

I had a list of them all,

but I left it at school."

"I saw the list," Cam said.

She closed her eyes and said, "Click!"

Cam always closes her eyes

and says, "Click!"

when she wants to remember something.

Cam has an amazing memory.

"My memory is like a camera," she says.

"I have a picture in my head

of everything I've seen.

Click! is the sound my camera makes."

Cam's eyes were still closed.

"I'm looking at the list," she said.

Then she opened her eyes.

She looked at all her friends

on the baseball field.

"Jane, Annie, and Evan were on the list.

They're not here yet."

Cam's real name is Jennifer.

But because of her great memory

people started calling her "the Camera."

Then "the Camera" became just "Cam."

Cam, Eric, and their friends waited.

Then Jane, Annie, and Evan

all came at the same time.

Robert and Rachel divided everyone

into two teams.

Then Robert called out,

"Play ball!"

2. HOME RUN!

Cam and Eric were on Robert's team.

They were on the field

at the start of the game.

The first batter hit the ball

high into the air.

Robert ran back.

He reached up and caught it.

"One out!" he called.

The next batter

hit the ball onto the ground.

Cam reached down for the ball.

She threw it to Eric at first base.

"Two outs!" Robert called.

Then Amy came to bat.

"Move back," Robert told his team.

Amy swung hard at the first pitch
and missed.

"Strike one!" Robert called.

Amy swung hard at the second pitch, too,
and missed.

"Strike two!" Robert called.

Amy held her bat.

She looked out at the pitcher and waited.

She swung hard at the third pitch.

She hit the ball high over Robert's head.

Amy ran to first base.

Robert ran back for the ball.

Amy ran to second base.

Robert kept running back.

Amy ran to third base.

Robert ran off the baseball field.

He ran past some children

who were flying kites.

Robert ran to where

people were sitting on benches

reading, talking, and resting.

He stopped and looked for the ball.

Amy ran home.

"Home run!" Amy shouted.

"I hit a home run!"

Amy and the others on her team cheered.

Rachel took the bat.

She stood at home plate.

Everyone waited for Robert

to throw the ball to the pitcher.

"Hurry! Hurry!" Rachel called.

"I want to hit a home run, too."

Robert ran back onto the field.

"I can't find it," he called.

"I can't find the ball!"

3. THERE IT IS

Cam closed her eyes and said, "Click!"

"The ball went over Robert's head," she said.

"It bounced near a tree."

Cam opened her eyes.

She pointed to a tree

at the edge of the baseball field.

"That's the one," she said.

Cam, Eric, and the others

ran to the tree.

They looked for the ball.

"I see it. I see it," Rachel said.

She ran past the tree

and picked something up.

"No, it's not the ball," she said.

"It's just a rolled-up piece of paper."

Dara pointed to something near a bench.

"There's a ball," she said.

"But it's not ours. It's red."

Eric looked at a puddle.

"This looks deep," he said.

"Maybe the ball is in here."

Eric found a branch on the ground.

He used it to poke in the puddle.

"It is deep," he said.

Eric kept poking.

"Hey!" he called out.

"I found something."

Eric used the branch

to push it out of the puddle.

"It's not the ball," Eric said.

"It's just an empty soda can."

"There it is," Robert said.

"I found it."

He pointed to a girl and boy

who were playing catch.

Robert said, "They're playing with

our ball."

4. THAT'S OUR BALL

The girl threw the ball high

over the boy's head.

The boy jumped,

but he didn't catch it.

He turned, ran,

and stopped the ball with his foot.

Just then Cam remembered something.

The boy picked the ball up.

Cam closed her eyes and said, "Click!"

Robert walked over to the girl and boy.

Eric, Rachel, and the others

followed him.

"That's our ball," Robert said.

"Amy hit it over my head

and you found it.

Now we want it back."

Cam opened her eyes.

She looked at the benches.

She looked at the people sitting on them.

Cam closed her eyes again

and said, "Click!"

"This ball is ours," the girl said.

"We brought it from home."

Robert held out his hand and said,

"Let me see it."

The girl gave the ball to Robert.

He showed it to Rachel.

"Is this yours?" he asked.

Rachel looked at the ball and said,

"No, it's not.

I wrote my name on the ball."

She gave the ball back to the girl.

"I'm sorry," Robert said.

"I was wrong. It's not our ball."

Rachel told Robert and the others,

"Let's keep looking."

"No," Cam said and opened her eyes.

"We don't have to look for the ball.

We have to look for a dog."

5. RUFF! RUFF!

"That's silly," Rachel said.

"We didn't lose a dog.

We lost a ball."

Cam led them to the red ball.

"I found that before," Dara said.

"It's not ours."

Eric told Cam, "Our ball is white."

Cam picked up the red ball.

She showed it to her friends.

"Do you see the teeth marks

in this ball?" she asked.

"An old man was playing catch

with his dog."

"That's right," Eric said.

"First the ball almost hit me.

Then the dog almost ran into me."

"This is all very nice," Rachel said.

"But I want to find my ball.

I want a chance to hit a home run, too."

Cam said, "I think the old man

threw this ball.

The dog ran for it.

But it took back Rachel's ball.

That's why this red ball was left

near the bench.

We should look for the dog.

It's small, brown, and has white spots.

If we find that dog,

we'll find Rachel's ball."

"No," Robert said. "Let's just

keep looking for Rachel's ball."

Robert and some of the children

kept looking for the ball.

Cam, Eric, Rachel, and Evan

looked for the dog.

They found it in the open field.

It was running to the old man.

There was a ball in its mouth.

Cam, Eric, Rachel, and Evan

ran to the old man, too.

The old man took the ball

out of the dog's mouth.

It was a white ball.

He was about to throw it.

"Stop!" Cam called to him.

"Don't throw the ball."

He stopped.

He didn't throw the ball.

"That's mine," Rachel told the man.

Cam gave him the red ball.

"This is yours," she said.

The old man looked at

the red and white balls.

"The white one has a name on it.

Are you Rachel?" the man asked.

"Yes," Rachel told him.

"Then this is yours," the man said.

He gave Rachel the white ball.

"I'm sorry we had it.

I wasn't watching what ball

Pal brought back."

Ruff! Ruff! Pal barked.

Rachel ran to Robert

and showed him the ball.

"You were right," Robert told Cam.

"Let's play ball," Rachel said.

She walked to home plate.

"Pitch it here," Rachel said.

"I want to hit a home run."

A Cam Jansen
Memory Game

Do you remember the picture on page 4?

Can you answer these questions?

1. Who is in front, Cam or Eric?

2. What color are Eric's sneakers?

3. How many dogs are in the picture?

4. Who is stepping in a puddle?